NIBBLES

the mostly mischievous monkey

Martha Myers

Pacific Press® Publishing Association

Nampa, Idaho

Oshawa, Ontario, Canada

www.pacificpress.com

Edited by Christy Yingling
Designed by Dennis Ferree
Cover art by Mary Rumford
Inside art by Mark Ford

Additional copies of this book are available by calling toll free
1-800-765-6955 or visiting http://www.adventistbookcenter.com

All Scripture quotations are taken from the *International
Children's Bible, New Century Version,* copyright © 1983,
1986, 1988 by Word Publishing, Dallas, Texas 75039. Used
by permission.

Library of Congress Cataloging-in-Publication Data

Myers, Martha, 1922-
    Nibbles, the mostly mischievous monkey/Martha Myers
    p. cm. — (Julius & friends; 10)
    Summary: When Jean tries to care for her new pet
squirrel monkey, she finds she needs patience and prayer.
    ISBN 0-8163-1947-2
    [1. Squirrel monkeys. 2. Monkeys as pets. 3. Pets
4. Christian life.] I.Title. II. Series.

PZ7.M9912 Ni 2002
—dc21   2002032992

02 03 04 05 06 • 5 4 3 2 1

Contents

Other Books in the Julius and Friends Series

CHAPTER

1

Surprise in the Mail

Jean, Allen, and their pets had just arrived home from a summer of fun and work on Dad's fishing boat. Dad had to fish several more weeks, so even though they knew they would miss him, it felt great to put their feet on solid ground, see friends, and, best of all, go shopping. They had earned money working for Dad and couldn't wait to spend it.

The pets acted happy too. Well, almost. Sailor the cat sat patiently waiting for his favorite toy-on-a-string to swing as it did on the boat.

Mitzie, the dachshund, waddled around on her sea legs, holding one foot up, then waiting for the ground to come up to meet it.

The parakeet, Purple Boy, didn't care where his cage hung. He still chattered, "Purple Boy. My name's Purple Boy. Pretty, pretty Purple Boy."

Mom sang as she went about her work, happier to be home than tossed about by the sea. She wasn't as adventurous as the children.

The next morning after breakfast and worship, Allen and Jean ran up the road to Aunt Nettie and Uncle's dairy farm. Aunt Nettie took care of the calves. She loved them, and they became her pets. Allen and Jean considered the calves their pets too. They helped Aunt Nettie feed them, then stopped and talked to Pansy, the old family cow. Uncle had lots of pretty little Jersey cows, but Pansy was special. She even let them ride on her back sometimes.

Allen and Jean helped Uncle pull down hay for the cows then ran home for the soup and sandwiches Mom had ready for them.

"We'll go shopping tomorrow," Mom promised. "Make a list of the things you really want to spend your money on."

"I know what I want," Allen said. "A special racecar."

"What do you do first?" Mom asked.

"I know," Jean said. "We take out our tithe and offering."

The next day Mom called "all aboard" for the mall! It took a long time to buy clothes with money they had earned, but at last they arrived back at the car. Mom was exhausted, but Allen and Jean had energy to spare.

At home, everything came out of the packages. Excitement filled the room along with shirts, jeans, sweaters, skirts, and socks. Allen didn't care much about the clothes, but he loved the racecar. It was red with white and black stripes. *Zooom,* look at it go!

"We have enough clothes here to last all year." Jean laughed. "Thanks for helping out, Mom." She held a skirt up to her waist and whirled around.

"What did you get special for yourself?" Mom asked.

"Oh, I know what I'm going to get."

Jean whirled again. "It's a surprise. I've ordered it already. It's something I've wanted a long time."

That night, when Jean helped Mom with supper, she showed her an advertisement of a tiny monkey that sat in a cup. "Look, Mom, isn't this just darling?"

"It's cute," Mom answered. "Now let's get supper on the table, OK?"

It was still a couple of days before school would start. They found their friends and caught up on all the news. Allen and Jean's summer differed from most because they spent it at sea on Dad's boat. They had shells and shark's teeth and stories to share with the others.

"You know what?" Allen said. "We saw a huge whale and her baby. They came right toward our boat! The mother looked like she'd crash into us."

"And just before she did," Jean continued the story, "she flipped that big tail. Splash! Down she went under our boat."

"The baby did just what the mother did," Allen said. "Only it didn't make such a big splash."

"Scary, I have to admit," Jean added.

School started with the excitement and flurry of all first days—new classes, new teachers, and even new students.

One day, while the children were at school, Mom heard the phone ring and hurried to answer. "Yes, yes, I'm coming," she mumbled. "Hello?"

"Hello, ma' am," a stranger's voice said. "Is this Jean Matthews?"

"No, it's her mother."

"Well, her monkey is here," the voice continued. "Would you pick him up right away? It's too cold for him here."

"Monkey?" Mom said. "We don't have a monkey."

"He's addressed to Jean Matthews. Please hurry."

Mom double-checked the address to make sure it was theirs.

"Well," she said. "It looks like we do have a monkey!"

CHAPTER

2

The Monkey Arrives

"Does he come with instructions?" Mom asked.

"This bag might have them." The clerk at the airport loosened the bag from the crate. A small slip of paper along with monkey treats, an apple, and a toy monkey dropped out.

"Not much here." Mom sighed. "I hope my daughter knows more about monkeys than I do."

The clerk laughed. "He's a strange looking monkey, isn't he?"

"All I can see is a ball of fur." Mom picked up the crate and headed for the car. She set it on the front seat beside her.

"Well, little fellow, hope you'll like us," Mom told the monkey. "You'll have lots to get used to, with all our other critters [animals]. You never know what might show up at our house. Know what I mean?" She chatted all the way home to comfort him.

At home, Mom put the crate on the desk. She offered the monkey a treat, but he wouldn't reach out for it. She couldn't help wondering how long he had been in the little box.

"I'll leave you right here until Jean comes. Won't she be surprised!"

When Jean came home, she hurried past the little crate into the kitchen. "Mom, may I go to Sylvia's to do some homework?"

"Not now," Mom said. "There's a package on the desk for you."

"For me?" Jean hurried back into the other room. Complete silence followed. Quite unusual. Mom walked in to see what had happened. Jean looked up. "How did he get here?"

"Someone from the airport called and wanted me to come right away to pick up our monkey. I told him we didn't have a monkey, but he insisted," Mom said.

"Oh, I didn't expect him so soon." Jean looked guilty.

"I would have waited for you, but they worried about the cold," Mom said.

"I'm sorry, Mom, I should have told you sooner."

"Jean, how could you get an animal like this without talking to us about it?" Mom asked.

Jean hung her head. "I told Dad I had wanted it for a long time."

"And he let you?"

"Well, he didn't say No." She looked ashamed.

"And you took that to mean Yes?" Mom asked.

"When we went to the store, Dad showed me where I could get a money order. I thought it would be OK."

"I see." Mom smiled. "You took advantage of Dad's soft heart. Right?"

"I guess I did," Jean said.

"You've taken on a big responsibility," Mom said. "We'll help, but you'll have to keep him out of trouble. Monkeys always mean trouble!"

Jean saw Allen coming and ran out to meet him. "Allen, the monkey came!" she called.

"He did? What did Mom say?"

"Not much. I'll tell you later. Come in and see him. He's really cute."

Allen and a couple of friends rushed inside. They peered through the slats of the crate and *oohed* and *aahed* at the little ball of fur inside.

"Can you take him out?" Allen asked.

"I don't know. Mom?" Jean called.

"What's the problem?"

"How can we get him out?"

"What if we unfasten the door, just a little?"

The monkey just stared. Mom pulled one end of a leash out of the cage and gave it to Jean, then opened the door wide. The monkey shifted on his perch. Jean pulled gently. Suddenly the monkey swung from the end of the leash. Everyone jumped back. What a surprise! This was no ball of fur! The monkey had a zucchini-like body with a long tail attached. A small head sat on his shoulders. His legs were long. At full height, he stood only about eight inches.

"Move slowly," Mom said. "Don't rush him." She wished she knew just what to expect of the monkey. *What would they do with him? Where could they keep him? In that small box?* Thoughts ran through Mom's mind while the children squealed with delight.

The monkey climbed the leash into Jean's hand, but when she tried to hold him, "Ouch! He bit me." Even though he had tiny teeth, it hurt.

"Looks like you've got lots of work ahead for you," Mom said.

"First thing," Jean decided, "I have to name him." That took some time. Nothing fit. At last she named him Nibbles because of the cute way he nibbled his food. Days of frustration followed. Jean couldn't find anything at the library on how to train a squirrel monkey. She had to learn from her mistakes. Mom suggested she wear heavy leather gloves. She made a little progress then. When Nibbles's teeth couldn't bite through the gloves, he looked slyly up at Jean as if to say, OK, you win this time.

Jean covered the chest by the window with layers of paper, then tied Nibbles to it. This gave him more space. At night she put him back in his crate.

Five-year-old Lori came to visit for a week. She fell in love with Nibbles. He rode on her shoulder or hung onto her hair or clothes. She quickly learned that Nibbles wouldn't bite if she didn't try to touch him with her hands.

One evening Mom was busy with supper when Lori stopped to watch. "Don't let that monkey in the pan." Mom laughed. "Or we'll have fried monkey for supper."

Lori jumped back. "We don't want that, do we, Nibs?"

Mom turned off the heat and took the pan to the sink. An awful smell followed her. She looked back. To her horror, there sat Nibbles—on the still-red stove element! She grabbed the leash and lifted him straight up off the stove. She reached for a clean towel and wrapped it gently around Nibbles. Then she called

Jean, who ran to see what had happened.

"Nibbles is burned." Mom handed him to Jean and reached for her keys. "Come on, Lori, let's get him to the vet."

Lori stood like a statue. Mom put her arm around her, and Lori began to cry. "I'm sorry. I didn't mean to let him get burned."

"It was an accident, honey. Come on, let's hurry," Mom said. "We'll pray for him on the way, OK?"

"OK," Lori said, but she sniffled all the while she climbed in the car and buckled her seat belt.

CHAPTER
3

Nibbles Gets Lost

"Well, what do we have here?" The vet looked at Nibbles. "Got into mischief, did he? That's a monkey for you." He continued to talk while he laid Nibbles on the table. Nibbles made no attempt to bite, nor did he make a sound. He finished the visit with his hind legs and his lower tail all bandaged.

"I've given him a shot to help stop infection," the vet said. "But bring him back in a couple of days for me to check."

Jean wanted to squeeze Nibbles tight but didn't dare.

For the next few days Nibbles looked miserable. "Poor baby," became a common phrase around the house. He didn't complain, though. Before long his bandages came off, and he seemed no worse for the experience.

"Nibbles didn't bite the vet when he held him," Jean said. "I wish I could hold him and dress him up. He'd look so sweet."

"Give him time," Mom assured her. "He can't resist your charm for long."

"Oh, Mom." Jean grinned.

"I have good news for you," Mom said one evening. "Dad will come home next week. He called this morning."

"Great!" Allen said. "I can show him my racecar."

"And he can see Nibbles!" Jean said. "How about that, little monkey?"

When Dad arrived, he asked about the monkey.

"Oh, he's so cute," Jean said. "But . . ."

"But what? Don't you like him?" Dad asked.

"Yes, but he bites," Jean complained.

"Doesn't look like that little thing could hurt." Dad shook his head. "Look at those tiny teeth."

"His bites sting for a long time," Jean told Dad.

Dad walked over to Nibbles. "What's this? His collar around his middle?"

"That's because he doesn't have a neck!"

"Come on, monkey," Dad said. "We must get acquainted."

Nibbles jumped on Dad's shoulder and curled up. Dad reached to get him down. Nibbles tried to teach Dad his "no touch" rule. He acted surprised to find himself in hands too tough to bite! After a few lessons, Nibbles learned better manners. He even learned to like having his tummy rubbed. He always stretched and twisted a little so no spots would get missed.

Jean watched and wished she could hold him like that.

"You do it now," Dad told her.

"But, Dad, he'll . . ."

"Try it."

Carefully Jean touched him, then gently rubbed the soft fur on his tummy. She smiled. "He didn't bite!"

"Now pick him up," Dad encouraged. Nibbles draped himself over Jean's hand. He rolled over, and she put her hand on his back. *"Chit, chit,"* he said, but he didn't bite.

"Oh, Dad, thanks!" Jean's eyes got bright and misty. "I've prayed and prayed! Now I'm finally holding him." Nibbles turned a couple of whirls around her arm, just to show her he didn't mind at all.

When the weather got warm, Jean tied Nibbles to the big apple tree in the backyard. With a longer leash he could have more freedom. The widespread branches made a perfect playground. Jean discovered Nibbles liked bugs. His favorite treats included spiders and ear-wigs. Grasshoppers topped the list. He held hoppers like people hold ice-cream cones. His eyes danced, and he smacked his lips as if to say, "Mmm, good."

"You can't guess what I saw Nibbles do!" Allen said. "He ran his leash through his hands, then jumped to the big branch that's by itself."

"So?" Jean asked.

"It looked like he measured the line."

"Come on, Allen. He couldn't do that!"

"I saw him," Allen insisted. Later Jean saw him do it again and decided that's just what he did.

When the snowball bush bloomed, Jean tied Nibbles to it. Each snowball has many tiny flowers that make one big flower. All kinds of bugs hide in them.

Nibbles went right to work on them. The snowball bush had branches full of little twigs. It didn't take long before Nibbles's leash got tangled. When this happened, he lost his temper. He squealed his angriest squeal and tore up all the flowers around him. Someone had to go out and untangle him. The pile of flowers on the grass made it easy to find him.

Dad made a big cage for Nibbles with a place for food and a couple of perches. Now Nibbles could do his favorite whirls on the monkey bars. He twirled around and around.

One day while Mom napped, Nibbles got out of his cage. When Jean came home from school, she missed him. "Mom, I can't find Nibbles. Where could he be?"

"Oh, honey, perhaps he's asleep somewhere."

"I've looked every place I can think of." Her eyes opened wide. "The door's open; he must have gone outside," Jean moaned.

"He's probably in the snowballs then," Mom said.

Jean searched the trees. No Nibbles. "Where could he go?"

"It's hard to say," Mom said. "He's so fast."

"He's too small to be out there by himself." Jean groaned. "I guess I'd better find Allen and maybe some others to help look for him."

"That's a good idea," Mom said. "Remember, Jean, God knows when a sparrow falls, and He knows about Nibbles."

"I know Mom. Let's pray that God will keep Nibbles safe and bring him home."

CHAPTER
4

Runaway Nibbles

Jean ran to the playground. "Allen, hurry! Nibbles is gone," she called.

Allen and his friends came to see what had happened. "What's wrong?"

"Nibbles is lost," Jean cried. "He must have gotten out the door."

"Maybe he's in the house asleep somewhere," Allen said.

"I've looked everywhere. Please help me find him!"

"Sure." Allen looked around. "He's so little. What do you want us to do?"

"First, we'll have to ask God to help us," Jean said.

They formed a circle, and Jean prayed, "Dear Jesus, You know when a sparrow falls. I know You know where Nibbles is. Please help us find him. Thank You. Amen."

The problem was where to look. They knew he might be anywhere. After some discussion, they decided to spread out and look in different directions.

"I don't think he'll go far," Allen said.

"He probably won't be on the ground, either," Jean added.

They searched the neighborhood. They looked by the hedges and fences. They called and listened, but found no Nibbles.

That evening Allen and Jean joined Mom on the porch.

"He's gone. We won't ever see him again," Jean sobbed.

"I thought Jesus would help us find him," Allen said.

"Now wait," Mom said. "Our prayers are not always answered the way we expect. God knows what's best, and we must ask His will."

"Wouldn't it be God's will to find Nibbles?" Jean asked. "He can't take care of himself out there!"

"We don't see things the way God does," Mom tried to explain. "Don't give up yet."

"Did you hear that?" Jean jumped up. *Squeak, squeak.* "Where did it come from?" They all listened.

"It sounds closer now," Allen said.

"There he is," Jean cried. "He's on the power line!"

"Look." Allen pointed. "He's turning whirlies on the high line."

"He'll get killed." Jean ran down the sidewalk, just as Nibbles jumped to the wire that came to the house.

"He's having a great time," Allen said. "How can he get hurt?"

"He won't," Mom said, "if he doesn't touch something from the ground."

A few more steps, a few more whirlies, and Nibbles leaned over the wire to squeak at Jean.

"Come on, Nibs, jump! Come to me," Jean cried. Nibbles hesitated, then made a flying leap and landed on Jean. "Nibbles, you're home safe. Thank You, Jesus," she whispered.

"Now that's funny," Allen laughed. "He looked like a flying squirrel except for that weird tail."

"Your tail's not weird, is it Nibbles?" Nibbles just gave a little squeak and curled up on Jean's shoulder. He tucked his head down into the soft fur on his tummy, like a bird puts his head under his feathers.

"Listen," Jean said. "Hear Nibbles purr?"

"Monkeys don't purr, silly," Allen said.

"What do you know about monkeys anyway?" Jean said. "I think he learned it from the cat."

Sometimes Jean gave Nibbles a small piece of candy. He'd do most anything for it. He'd squeal and beg and even grab the bag.

Mom didn't allow Nibbles loose in the house except in Jean's room. After Jean had a mole taken off her back, the doctor gave her pills to take. She opened the bottle, and Nibbles swooped down and grabbed it. He tried to shove the pills in his mouth but instead scattered them across the room.

"You naughty monkey!" Jean cried. "Look what you've done. You've spilled my medicine. Now what will I do?" Nibbles squeaked softly from the curtain. He dropped the empty bottle and jumped down on Jean and started to purr.

"Just for that, you can stay in your cage all day," Jean scolded. "Even if you are sorry."

She hurried off to school. Nibbles rattled his door.

"Well, Nibbles, I don't know what you did," Mom said, "but it looks like you're grounded." Nibbles jumped up and down and squealed at the top of his voice.

"Sorry, those are orders from the boss," Mom said.

When Jean got home, she bounded up the steps.

"Hey, Jean," Allen yelled, "come play ball with us."

"OK, just a minute." She dropped her books on the table and went to say Hi to Nibbles. *Where is he?* she thought. *How did he get out? Oh, he's on the bottom of the cage.*

"Nibbles, what's wrong? Mom!" she screamed, "Nibbles is dead!"

"Oh, Jean, don't panic." Mom looked at Nibbles sprawled out on the floor of his cage.

"He's alive, honey," Mom said. "At least he's breathing. Take him out and see if he's hurt."

"You don't think those pills would hurt him, do you?"

"Pills?" Mom gasped. "What pills?"

CHAPTER
5

Surprise!

"Nibbles grabbed the bottle when I took a pill this morning," Jean explained. "He ran up the curtain and spilled them. Then he tried to shove them in his mouth."

"In that case," Mom said, "let's call the doctor and see what he thinks."

"A monkey took the pills! A monkey?" The doctor laughed. "This is the first time I've had a monkey for a patient."

"He probably thought they were candy," Mom told him.

"They won't hurt him," the doctor said between laughs. "He'll be drugged for a while. Just move him around now and then and let him sleep it off."

"Jean, I thought you would come and play ball." Allen burst in. "What's wrong with Nibbles?"

"He's drugged from my pills." Jean said.

"Look at him," Allen said. "He sure acts weird."

Since Jean knew Nibbles would survive, she admitted he acted funny. When they put him on the floor, he didn't walk straight. He stretched out on the floor and rolled his glazed eyes around, not able to focus on anything. Whenever he tried to get up, he'd just fall over and lie on his back, looking foolish.

"You know it really isn't funny," Jean said. "Mom, will these pills make me act that way?"

"Of course not." Mom hugged Jean. "You take a certain amount for a specific reason. The doctor prescribed that medicine just for you."

"You wouldn't take Nibbles's medicine," Dad added.

"Yuck," Jean grimaced, "I sure don't want his pills."

"You don't want any pills from anyone," Dad reminded her, "unless it's from someone who takes care of you."

"I know," Jean said. "Just say No!"

Nibbles got well and became his old mischievous self. "If you had seen how silly you acted," Jean told him, "you'd never want to help yourself to anything again."

Whenever Jean took Nibbles and Mitzie the dog for a walk, Nibbles hopped on Mitzie's back. He looked like a miniature cowboy urging his horse to go faster. Nibbles held on to Mitzie's collar, which put his head down close to hers. Nibbles's little pointed ears looked like they blew in the wind. His long legs made him taller in back, like he stood in the stirrups. Mitzie just waddled along, not in a hurry.

The two got a lot of attention. However, if Nibbles got more than his share, Mitzie sat down. That made it hard for Nibbles to stay on her back.

One day they met Mrs. Brown. She thought they were so cute that she asked Jean to bring them to Sabbath School to show the kindergarten children.

"I don't know if I can," Jean told her. "I'll ask my parents and let you know."

She surprised the family when she told them about Mrs. Brown. Mom thought Nibbles might become frightened and bite someone. Dad didn't think Jean could handle both pets, but Allen thought it was a great idea.

Could he go with her?

"Suppose I just took Nibbles," Jean asked.

"That might work," Dad said, "if you took him in the bird cage."

Jean called Mrs. Brown and made arrangements for next Sabbath.

"Children, I have a surprise for you today," Mrs. Brown told them. Jean waited outside the door with Nibbles in the bird cage. When Mrs. Brown invited them in, the children became excited. They had never seen a monkey in Sabbath School before.

"That's Nibbles," one little boy spoke up. "I know him." When Mrs. Brown got them quieted down, she introduced Jean and Nibbles. All at once Jean felt scared. All the children waited for her to say something. Jean hadn't thought about what she would say.

Mrs. Brown came to her rescue. "Tell us about your little monkey."

"Well, uh—he—" Jean stammered.

Squeal, squeal, tut, tut, Nibbles complained. He rattled the door of his cage. Jean snapped the leash on and let him out. He climbed hand over hand up the leash. He stopped halfway up to watch the children, then climbed into Jean's hand. Jean relaxed and gave Nibbles a cracked peanut to work on.

She told them he lived in a big cage her dad had made. He only went free in her room; otherwise he was on a leash.

"We pray for him a lot because he always gets burned or lost or sick from eating something he shouldn't. Dad says to remember Nibbles isn't naughty, he's just a monkey.

"He can't stand anything that has a lid, like a bottle or a box. If he can't open it, he throws it on the floor and has a temper tantrum. We know Jesus takes care of him because he's still here."

Jean picked up the nut shells and put Nibbles back in the cage.

"What do we say to Jean and Nibbles?" Mrs. Brown asked.

"Thank you," they said. "Come again and bring Nibbles."

* * *

Early one morning, Nibbles's angry screams filled the air. "He is tangled in the snowball flowers again!" Jean sighed when she found her pet.

"Calm down, Nibs," Jean coaxed. "How can I untangle you?"

In a frenzy, Nibbles tore up the snowball flowers and dropped them on Jean.

"Nibs, stop it," she scolded.

Nibbles's screams continued.

"There, now, I've got you," Jean said, working to unhook the leash. "Just a minute, I'll have you free."

Swish, Nibbles jumped high into the tree. "Now look at you," Jean said. "OK, I'll just leave you there if that's what you want."

CHAPTER
6

Nibbles Goes Visiting

Jean ran into the house. "Mom," she called, "Nibbles got loose in the trees again." She grabbed her books and left for school.

I wonder what she wants me to do about it? Mom thought. She looked and saw Nibbles on the highest branches, his hands busy picking bugs and shoving them in his mouth. Happy little *"chit, chit"* sounds floated down. *"Squeak, squeak,"* Nibbles said when he saw Mom.

"Having a good time?" Mom asked. "Those bugs must taste yummy." Not knowing what else to do, she left the door open to make it easier for Nibbles to get in.

About an hour later Nibbles noticed the open door. He raced across the lawn, up the porch, and slipped inside. His cage door stood open too. Silently he went in. He got that drink of water he needed. Bug hunting made him thirsty. Now he felt so good he twirled around his perch and sounded a few *twit twits*.

Mom heard and hurried to shut the door, but she wasn't fast enough. Before she could say Stop, Nibbles jumped across the table, sprang to the curtain, and flew out the door. He scrambled across the lawn and up the tree to safety.

Jean came home and found him still in the trees. "Did you have a good day,

Nibs?" she called. Nibbles came closer to Jean. Chattering softly, he jumped to her.

"I do believe you're glad to see me!" Jean hugged him. She ran in the house, Nibbles on her shoulder, with his tail wrapped around her neck. He made soft little squeaks and purred in her ear.

"I think I'll let him out sometimes," Jean said. "He didn't run away, and he's happy. He got his tummy full for sure."

After that, most warm days found Nibbles out in the trees eating bugs. Then Nibbles began to explore the neighborhood. Two little boys, Rick and Gary Smith, lived next door. They had a big backyard with swings and a sandbox to play in. One day when they played in the sand, they heard *"chit, chit"* from the top of the patio.

"Oh, look, Gary," Rick said, "Nibbles is loose."

"Mama," they called.

Nibbles decided to join them. He slid down the patio post and onto Gary's shoulder. Gary's eyes got big, and he froze like an icicle. Mama came to the door. "Don't be frightened," she said, "I don't think he'll hurt you."

"But, Mama," Gary cried, "how will I get him off?"

"He's purring," Rick said. "Listen."

"Sure enough," Mama said, "he must be happy." Mama reached her arm out and tried to coax Nibbles off Gary.

Just then Jean came around the corner looking for Nibbles. "There you are, you little rascal," she said. Nibbles jumped to Jean and continued to purr.

"Here," Jean said, "I'll show you how to handle him." Jean sat down beside the boys with Nibbles. "When you want to move him, just pick him up by his tail like this." Jean lifted him from his comfortable position. The boys laughed when Nibbles climbed up his own tail into Jean's hand.

"Can we play with him?" Rick asked.

"If you don't grab him," Jean explained.

"We won't scare you, Nibbles," Gary promised.

"Daddy says we can have a monkey when Jesus comes," Rick said. "He'll be real tame."

"He says I can have a big fish," Gary added. "One I can pet and even ride on." His eyes shone when he thought of Jesus coming.

Jean smiled. She knew the boys had a beautiful aquarium in their home, full of the prettiest fish she had ever seen.

Rick and Gary took turns rubbing Nibbles's tummy. Nibbles stretched out and rolled a little so they wouldn't miss a spot. Oh, how he purred.

"I didn't know monkeys purred," their mama said.

"We aren't sure they do." Jean laughed. "We think he learned it from sleeping with the cat."

During the warm summer days, Nibbles visited the boys often. They were happy to have him come. Their mama knew when Nibbles arrived by the giggling and squealing she heard in the backyard.

One day Mr. Smith came home for lunch. He sank into his favorite chair and opened the newspaper. No one knew that Nibbles had gone inside the house to look around. Without warning, Nibbles jumped on Mr. Smith's shoulder.

Gary and Rick laughed. "Just take him by the tail, Daddy," Rick said.

"You boys stay back," Daddy said. "I'll take care of this."

"But, Daddy—"

"Never mind," Daddy said. "Just stay out of the way."

When Jean came home for lunch, the doorbell rang. "I'll get it," she called. She opened the door. There stood Mr. Smith, looking over the top of his open newspaper. Nibbles perched on his shoulder, his tail wrapped around Mr. Smith's neck. Nibbles leaped to Jean with a happy squeak.

Mr. Smith grinned. "I didn't know what else to do with him."

"I'm sorry he bothered you," Jean said.

"No bother. I'm just glad he's a friendly little fellow."

CHAPTER 7

Nibbles Rides a Horse

A shrill sound filled the air. "Wonder what that is?" Allen asked.

"It doesn't sound like Nibbles," Jean said.

A deep *"woof, woof"* mixed with the sound. "That's Barny," Allen said. "I know that sound."

Barny, a Saint Bernard dog, lived in a big fenced yard at the back of the vacant lot. The children had never gotten acquainted with him. Allen went in the house, but Jean walked slowly past the neighbors' houses. When she came to the empty lot, she saw Barny. Nibbles stood on a fence post just inches above that wide open mouth. He jumped up and down and shook his fists. He screeched to the top of his voice. Jean had never heard Nibbles scream like that.

"Nibbles!" she yelled. Nibbles didn't hear her call. Jean rushed into the tall grass and the blackberry bushes. They caught her clothes and scratched her legs and arms, and even pulled her hair. It didn't matter. Nibbles needed her help.

"Please don't let Barny get Nibbles," she prayed as she hurried through the brambles. She got within a few feet of him and called again. Still he jumped and screeched. Suddenly he leaped onto Jean's shoulder.

"What do you think you are doing?" she cried. "Do you want to be swallowed alive?"

Jean picked her way back to the street. Her arms and legs bled. Thorny branches stuck to her clothes.

"What happened to you?" Allen asked when she got home.

"I had to go through some berry bushes to get Nibbles," she said, near tears.

"You'd better come and get washed up," Mom said. "Then we'll put something on those scratches."

Nibbles settled down for a nap. After all, it had been an exciting day.

"I wonder," Jean said, "did Nibbles tease Barny, or did Barny scare him?"

"Guess you'll never know," Allen laughed.

"Probably Nibbles ran along the fence and Barny spotted him," Jean decided.

"Why didn't he leave?" Allen asked. "He's fast enough to get away from Barny!"

"You would think so," Jean agreed. "That's why I thought Nibbles might have teased Barny."

All this talk made Jean wonder what Nibbles did while he roamed the neighborhood. Mrs. Wilson had called once when she saw him in her apple tree. Sometimes someone would mention seeing him.

"Mrs. Martin told me he was on her windowsill," Allen said. "She talked to him through the glass and told him to go home." Allen laughed.

"One time she told me Nibbles sassed her." Jean giggled. "He probably did too. I'm glad she likes him."

"She thinks he's cute, even when he's naughty," Allen said. "She knows he's just a monkey!"

One day, when Jean walked past the dining-room window, she saw two boys at the Martins' place. She wondered what was going on because the Martins were gone. One boy stood on the ground and another on the roof, both looking up.

"What can those boys be doing?" Jean asked.

"There's one in the tree too," Allen exclaimed.

"Nibbles," Jean cried. "They're after Nibbles."

Jean went out onto the porch. Nibbles suddenly appeared over the fence. He raced across the ground, skidded around the corner of the house, and leaped onto Jean's shoulder.

Moments later the boys came in sight. They stopped short when they saw Jean and Nibbles.

"Is that your monkey?"

"He sure is," Jean said.

"We just tried to catch him."

"I'm glad you didn't." Jean grinned. "He might have bitten you."

"That little thing?" They walked away, laughing.

Another day, Jean decided to introduce Nibbles to her horse, Buddy. She loved riding him; why wouldn't Nibbles? She went to the pasture and got Buddy. She brushed him well and brought him to the house, then ran in to get Nibbles.

"Come on, Nibs," she said, snapping the leash onto his collar. "Want to ride a real horse?"

Nibbles, always ready for anything, perched on her shoulder and wrapped his tail securely around her neck. *"Squeak, squeak."* He let Jean know he thought it a fine idea.

"Here, Buddy," Jean said, "meet Nibbles." Nibbles offered a friendly squeal. Buddy curled his lip, showed his teeth, and then threw his head up and whinnied.

Jean pulled his head down, but Buddy turned away and refused to look at Nibbles. By this time Nibbles was excited. He showed his tiny teeth and squealed at Buddy.

"OK, enough!" Jean said, "Nibbles can ride anyway."

She put her hand through the loop on Nibbles's leash and jumped on the horse. Nibbles acted a little afraid, but Jean soothed him. He left her shoulder and jumped into her hands. Buddy danced around, and Nibbles squealed. Jean spoke softly to Buddy and patted him on the neck.

"Here, Nibbles, hold on to this." Jean gave him strands of Buddy's beautiful mane. With happy little *"chit chits"* and a squeal or two, off they trotted.

"This is much better than pokey Mitzie, right, Nibbles? Now you're a real cowboy," Jean assured him.

"If I made cowboy clothes, would you leave them on?" Jean asked Nibbles. "You're so cute when I dress you up. Why won't you keep the clothes on?"

A new neighbor came to the door one evening. "Do you folks have a monkey?" she asked.

"Sure," Allen said, "come in. Jean!" he yelled.

Jean came into the room. "Hi." She smiled.

"I'm Mrs. Jones from the street behind you. There's a monkey on my drapes!"

CHAPTER

8

More Monkeys

"That's got to be Nibbles." Jean laughed. "I'm sorry he bothered you," she said. "I'll go back with you and get him."

"I just didn't know what to do." Mrs. Jones laughed too. "He's really cute, but it's a surprise to find a monkey on the drapes!"

"I can catch him by the tail," Jean explained, "or coax him to me. Sometimes it takes a little candy, which I carry with me."

When they arrived at the house, Nibbles hung from the curtain rod, watching out the window. He made a happy squeak and jumped onto Jean's shoulder.

"Nibbles, what am I supposed to do with you?" Jean scolded. "You act like you own the whole neighborhood."

She brought Nibbles home and put him in his cage.

"I'll leave you there for the whole week," Jean told him. "Maybe then you'll learn to stay home!"

"Oh, Jean, there's a picture of a couple of squirrel monkeys in the paper," Mom said.

Jean picked up the paper and turned the page. "How darling." She laughed. "One's wrapped in a blanket. 'Apartment Fire Turns Into a Lot of Monkey Business,' " she read the headline. "Looks like they attacked the firefighter."

"Let's see." Allen grinned. "They sure look like Nibbles, don't they?"

"Firefighters had to battle one of the monkeys as well as the fire," Jean read.

"That must have been a surprise for the firefighters." Allen said.

"Guess the one monkey hadn't been tamed," Jean added.

"Can't you just see Nibbles in a room with a fire?" Allen grinned.

"Then to have those funny-looking firefighters rush in with their hoses." Jean laughed. "Nibbles is tame, but he still gets a little wild when he's frightened."

"I think maybe it's about time for a trip to the zoo," Mom said that night at supper. "How about tomorrow?"

"Great!" Allen shouted as he jumped up and down.

"Oh, thanks, Mom," Jean said. "I've been thinking about it because you said we'd go soon."

The zoo had something for everyone. First, they looked in on the deer and antelope. They watched the lions and tigers and leopards.

"Nibbles would like a big cat like that," Allen said.

"Oh, look at the babies," Jean cried. "They look so cuddly."

"You can't cuddle them now, Jean," Mom said. "That will have to wait!"

"Just think, when Jesus comes, they can all be pets."

The big gorilla sat in his rubber tire and scowled at them.

"He sure doesn't look cuddly," Allen said.

Finally, they came to Monkey Island. On the highest point sat a little schoolhouse. They watched the monkeys quarrel over which one would ring the bell.

"They're like one big family," Jean said. Some played tag, some fished peanuts out of the water, some slept, while others just sat and scratched.

Next, they found the squirrel monkeys. Lots of squirrel monkeys! Many were in a screened-in porch. They could go back and forth into a large room inside the building.

First, they watched the monkeys playing outside.

"Oh, Allen," Jean squealed, "look at those babies on their mother's backs!"

"They sure have to hang on tight when Mama makes a flying leap." Allen laughed.

"I'd like to bring Nibbles and show him all these relatives," Jean exclaimed.

On the way home, Allen and Jean compared Nibbles to the monkeys they had just seen.

"Did you notice anything different about them?" Mom asked.

"They sure looked alike," Allen said. "And they seemed to have a good time together."

"I think Nibbles has softer eyes," Jean said. "That was one of the first things I noticed."

"I thought that too," Mom said. "Nibbles has learned about love. I think that's the difference."

"Nibbles had a wild look when we first got him," Jean remembered.

"The monkeys were fun," Allen said, "but I sure laughed at those hippos."

"They were so big and ugly." Jean made a face.

"When they caught those big cabbages the keeper threw at them, crunch, they disappeared." Allen whistled.

"Imagine a mouth big enough to catch a cabbage!" Jean said.

The next morning Jean got up early and found a big black cat curled up on Nibbles's cage. The cat jumped to the floor and streaked out the dog door.

"Well," Jean said, "how long has this been going on?" Whenever anyone came down early, they saw the black cat and knew Nibbles had had company during the night.

"Wonder who the cat belongs to?" Jean said. "I never see him around any other time."

"Nibbles probably met him on one of his trips around the neighborhood," Allen guessed.

Since school was out, almost everyone had gone on vacation. Dad was out on the fishing boat. Jean and Allen sort of ran out of things to do.

"You know what I'd like?"

"What?" Allen said, ready for any suggestion.

"A camping trip," Jean said.

"Do you think Mom would take us?"

"Let's ask," Jean said.

"Mom, Mom," they shouted and ran into the house.

"What's all the excitement?" Mom asked.

"Will you take us camping? Please, Mom, please?"

CHAPTER
9

Nibbles Meets the Squirrels

"Camping? I don't know much about camping," Mom said. "Dad's not home, and I don't think I could do that without his help."

"I wish Dad could stay home in the summer," Allen complained. "Jimmy's dad takes them camping lots of times."

"Allen, you know Dad can't help being gone," Jean scolded. "He would rather stay home too. But he makes money for our family by fishing every summer in Alaska."

"I know. I'm sorry. I just miss him."

"We all do, Allen." Mom sighed.

"I camped with the Pathfinders, Mom," Jean said hopefully. "I can build a fire and everything."

"Yes, and she can make soup on the fire and even pitch a tent," Allen added.

"A tent?" Mom asked. "We don't have a tent."

"There's a big canvas in the shed," Jean said. "We could fix it for a tent."

"What would you do with Nibbles and Mitzie?"

"Take them with us," the children chorused.

"Oh, I don't know." Mom worried. "I don't like to go without Dad."

"Just for a couple of days? We'll do all the work," Jean promised.

Mom looked at the children. They wanted to go so badly. Mom had grown up where there were no forests and a person could see all around. The children didn't know that forests frightened her. She had kept her fears hidden.

"I'll have to think about it," she said.

After worship that evening, she agreed to take them if they would help. Together they made a list of what they needed.

The canvas was heavier and bigger than they thought. They pulled and tugged and got it into the station wagon. At last they were loaded and ready to go.

"Everyone buckled up?" Mom asked. "Allen, will you pray for God's protection on our trip?"

"Thank You, Jesus," Allen prayed, "for letting us go camping. Please keep us safe. Amen. Oh, yes, bless Dad, too."

They arrived at the campground just in time to find the last campsite. Nibbles traveled in a bird cage. Mitzie was on her leash. Jean put Nibbles, bird cage and all, on the table. She turned her attention to getting the canvas tent up.

A monkey doesn't go unnoticed, and before long, several children gathered around the table. Nibbles put on the best show possible in such a small space. He turned around and around on his perch, chattering at the children. The more they laughed and clapped, the more he turned. He rattled the door to get out. Parents came to see what the children were doing and stayed to watch.

"Now it's your turn, Nibbles," Jean exclaimed. She opened the little door of the cage and snapped Nibbles's leash on him. Everyone jumped back because they didn't know what to expect.

"He won't bite unless he's really frightened," Jean told them. "Nibbles, these are your camper friends."

Nibbles chirped a couple of happy noises as the children came closer to him. They felt the soft fur on his tummy. He held a finger in his hand and pulled a little girl's ribbon. They giggled when he touched them. Jean added a rope to his leash and tied him to a fir tree. Much to her surprise, Nibbles flattened his body against the tree and zigzagged his way up until the rope stopped him.

Word must have spread fast to the squirrels in the woods to come and check out this strange-looking squirrel. They chattered together like long-lost relatives.

"The squirrels' bodies are almost the same as Nibbles's," Jean noticed.

"Except Nibbles's tail is like a rope, and the squirrels' are like dusters." Allen laughed.

After supper they gathered around the fire for worship. Smoky haze from many campfires blew around them. Nibbles curled up on Jean's shoulder and purred in her ear.

"Remember how Nibbles surprised us when we first heard him purr?" Jean asked.

"Sometimes Nibbles's purr is soft; other times he's so loud he rattles," Allen added. "He must have had a good day because I can hear him way over here."

"I thought for worship tonight we might talk about angels," Mom said. "It would be nice to invite them to camp with us, don't you think?"

"Do angels camp?" Allen asked.

"Sure." Jean quoted from Psalm 34:7, " 'The Lord saves those who fear him. His angel camps around them.' "

"Guess I never thought of it that way," Allen said.

They spent the evening telling stories of angels. They all remembered times they felt angels had protected them.

The campfire burned low, and the sleeping bags felt warm and snug. Nibbles crawled in with Jean, and Mitzie snuggled in with Allen. They each tied their pets' leashes to their wrists to keep the pets from exploring by themselves! Soon all fell asleep, except Mom, who found it hard to get comfortable.

Mom's eyes popped open. *It's daylight already,* she thought. *How did I ever go to sleep? What's that dark shadow? No, it can't be a bear.* She peered intently. It was a bear!

"Jean," Mom hissed. "A bear." Mom poked her with her elbow. "Jean, a bear!" She poked her again.

Jean groaned and rolled over. "Mom?"

"Just look," Mom whispered.

Jean rubbed her eyes and looked just in time to see the bear turn and go over the hill.

CHAPTER
10

Uninvited Camper

"Bear!" Jean yelled.

She and Allen ran toward the commotion over the hill. Mom and the pets followed. Nibbles hopped on Mitzie's back, screeching and chattering in the excitement. Mom put the pets in the car out of the way.

"Look, Mom," Allen said, "the bear jumped up on the car!"

"Those campers chased him off," Jean added.

Mom looked surprised. Big muddy

tracks led right to the windshield and smeared the glass. The wiper was broken.

"He must have been after the food," Mom said. They had put the food inside to keep it from the animals. She remembered how she had looked longingly at the car seat when they set up camp. She had tried to persuade the children to sleep in the station wagon.

"Wow," Allen interrupted her thoughts. "What if we had been asleep inside, with that bear on the hood?"

"We sure got off to an exciting start today." Jean giggled, then ran off to get Nibbles.

"Yes, and I'm hungry," Allen announced. "Let's eat."

"We'll eat, then we'll pick up camp and start for home," Mom decided.

"Oh, no," Allen groaned. "You wouldn't let a little old bear scare you off, would you?"

"Mom, we haven't had a chance to go to the falls," Jean complained. "Can't we stay another day, please?"

"You want to stay when you know a bear is roaming around?" Mom asked, surprised.

The ranger came by and told them not to worry. They had chased the bear farther into the woods.

"We have the angels camping with us," Jean said.

"Besides, the bear hasn't hurt anyone," Allen added.

"We'll stay on one condition," Mom said. "If I see the bear again, we're leaving. Agreed?"

The sun shone warm into the campsite. Mom and the pets stayed in camp. The neighboring campers took the children to the falls. Mom kept a little fire going and enjoyed the animals, especially Nibbles and the curious squirrels.

Nibbles zig-zagged up the tall tree as far as he could go. The squirrels zig-zagged the same way, but kept just out of Nibbles's reach. They scampered around, chattering back and forth with Nibbles. The squirrels had never seen anything like Nibbles. He acted much like they did, but his short fur and skinny tail looked quite different.

Jean and Allen were starved when they came back from their hike to the falls. Mom tied Nibbles and Mitzie to a camp chair while she started supper. She could grab the chair if they started to leave. Jean and Allen went to get sticks to roast Big Franks. Mom soon had everything ready on the table.

"Supper's ready," she called. "Come and get it."

The bushes at the side of the camp moved.

"OK, supper is on."

A bear stepped out of the bushes right in front of her! Mitzie lunged forward. Mom grabbed the chair and stepped on the leash at the same time. Mitzie choked, but it stopped her. Mom picked up the leash and held on tight. Nibbles, who had been taking a nap on Mitzie's back, tumbled into the dust. He squealed and raced up to Mom's shoulder. He stood his full height and waved his fists at the bear.

Mom could hardly believe the horrible growl that came from Mitzie. The bear stood calmly in the midst of the commotion. He looked for a long time at that crazy dog, then at Mom. Mom pulled tightly on Mitzie's leash. The bear's glance lingered on Nibbles, who still screamed at him.

The bear took a long look at the table. Had the cooking smells brought him here?

"Supper ready?" Allen and Jean bounced into camp, tumbling over each other when they saw the bear. The bear turned and disappeared back into the bushes.

"Are you all right?" Allen took Mitzie, still lunging and growling. Jean reached for Nibbles and pushed Mom into the chair.

"Let's eat supper," Mom gasped. "Then we're going home."

Getting packed didn't take long, and soon they were headed down the mountain. A sudden downpour made them remember the broken windshield wiper. They stopped to wait for a break in the rain.

"That bear couldn't catch Nibbles." Allen laughed. "I know why he didn't get Mom and Mitzie."

"Because we invited the angels to camp with us," Jean stated firmly.

"Well, I've had all the camping I want for a while," Mom said.

"The ranger said they had sent for someone at the zoo to come and catch the bear," Allen said. "Do you think we'll know him?"

"I doubt it." Jean hugged Nibbles. "Guess what I did just before we left?"

"With you, it's hard to tell." Allen chuckled. "What did you do?"

Jean grinned. "I left a big gob of honey on the table for the bear."

If you enjoyed this book,
you'll enjoy these other books in the
Julius and Friends series:

Julius, the Perfectly Pesky Pet Parrot
VeraLee Wiggins.
0-8163-1173-0. US$6.99, Cdn$11.49.

Tina, the Really Rascally Red Fox
VeraLee Wiggins.
0-8163-1321-0. US$6.99, Cdn$11.49.

Skeeter, the Wildly Wacky Raccoon
VeraLee Wiggins.
0-8163-1388-1. US$6.99, Cdn$11.49.

Lucy, the Curiously Comical Cow
Corinne Vanderwerff.
0-8163-1582-5. US$5.99, Cdn$9.99.

Thor the Thunder Cat
VeraLee Wiggins.
0-8163-1703-8. US$6.99, Cdn$11.49.

Prince, the Persnickety Pony
Heather Grovet.
0-8163-1787-9. US$6.99, Cdn$11.49.

Prince Prances Again
Heather Grovet.
0-8163-1807-7. US$6.99, Cdn$11.49.

Petunia, the Ugly Pug
Heather Grovet,
0-8163-1871-9, US$6.99, Cdn$11.49

Order from your ABC by calling **1-800-765-6955**,
or get online and shop our virtual store at
www.adventistbookcenter.com.

• Read a chapter from your favorite book.
• Order online.
• Sign up for email notices on new products.

Real-life lessons from the Bible for today's kids

Shoebox Kids Bible Stories
Jerry D. Thomas. As Sammy, Jenny, Willie, DeeDee, Chris and Maria meet at church, they find that their Bible stories have a strange way of fitting into the things that happen to them each week! Their adventures will help your child learn how the Bible makes a difference at home, at school, or on the playground.

1. **Creation to Abraham** Creation, the Sabbath, Cain and Abel, the Flood, Abraham and Isaac. Every chapter is a double story—one from the Bible, then a Shoebox story that applies the Bible lesson. Paper, 128 pages. 0-8163-1823-9.

2. **From Isaac to the Red Sea** The Bible stories in this book start with Eliezar's search for a wife for Isaac, include Joseph's dreams, and end with the parting of the Red Sea and bread from heaven. Paper, 128 pages. 0-8163-1877-8.

3. **From the Ten Commandments to Jericho** Water from the rock, the Ten Commandments, the golden calf, the brass serpent, Balaam's donkey, and crossing the Jordan. Paper, 128 pages. 0-8163-1911-1.

4. **From Joshua to David, Goliath, and Jonathan** Joshua gets tricked by the Gibeonites, the day the sun stood still, Samson defeats the Philistines, and David battles Goliath. Paper, 128 pages. 0-8163-1949-9.

Order from your ABC by calling **1-800-765-6955**, or get online and shop our virtual store at **www.adventistbookcenter.com**.

- Read a chapter from your favorite book
- Order online
- Sign up for email notices on new products

Meet Sarah Barnes—
an Adventist girl

These stories about a young pioneer girl named Sarah Barnes take children back in time to the days of William Miller between 1842 and 1844. Even as Sarah's family accepts the message of Jesus' soon return, Sarah must keep up with her daily chores and schoolwork. This four-book historical series will entertain and educate children about the Adventist heritage and hope.
US$6.99, Can$11.49 each.

1. A Song for Grandfather
Eight-year-old Sarah Barnes can't wait to see Grammy and especially Grandfather! She knows he'll tell her wonderful stories of his life as a sea captain. But Grandpa surprises the whole family with some startling ideas he heard William Miller preach from the Bible. *Jesus will return very soon and the world will come to an end!* Will they accept the message? Paper, 96 pages. 0-8163-1873-5.

2. Miss Button and the Schoolboard
Sarah and her best friend Pam love school – except for those annoying boys and that mean girl Nickie Cooper! Their beloved teacher, Miss Button, is the best teacher in the world. Even so, it's getting harder to be a Millerite and the teasing gets worse. Paper, 96 pages. 0-8163-1874-3.

3. A Secret in the Family
As the Barnes family looks eagerly for the return of Jesus on March 21, 1844, Ma and Pa surprise Sarah with an unexpected announcement: Ma's going to have a baby! Sarah's happy, yet confused. If the world is coming to an end, how does a baby fit into the plan? Paper, 96 pages. 0-8163-1887-5.

4. Sarah's Dissappointment
Sarah hears Samuel Snow preach that Jesus will definitely return on October 22, 1844. Good news! New hope! Still, it's a hard time for Sarah. Some of her friends are now her enemies. Paper, 96 pages. 0-8163-1888-3.